Return to Albemore

LYNN MICHELLE

Copyright © 2022 by Lynn Michelle.

ISBN 978-1-958678-42-8 (softcover)
ISBN 978-1-958678-43-5 (ebook)
Library of Congress Control Number: 2022915109

All rights reserved. No part of this book may be reproduced or transmitted in any form or by any means, electronic or mechanical, including photocopying, recording, or by any information storage and retrieval system without express written permission from the author, except in the case of brief quotations embodied in critical reviews and certain other noncommercial uses permitted by copyright law.

This book is a work of fiction. Names, characters, places, and incidents are the product of the author's imagination or are used fictitiously. Any resemblance to actual locales, events, or persons, living or dead, is purely coincidental.

Printed in the United States of America.

Book Vine Press
2516 Highland Dr.
Palatine, IL 60067

For Carol and Albert Trim
Always in My Heart

Chapter 1

I'm a horse; a wild mare, in fact. I have a long white flowing mane and a long white flowing tail. I'm a darker color than my mother, but she told me that I turn white when I grow up. Many things happen for a reason and I always wonder about that. Let me tell you a story about my life, it might help you learn.

It all started when I was born and grew up in the wild. I was born in the spring, on a beautiful green plain. I looked just like my mother but a little different since my mane and tail were small.

I struggled to get up so I could follow my mother and the herd. My mother waits for me patiently. When I got up my left hoof gave in and I fell to the green grass. I tried again and the same thing happened. My mother showed me how to get up without falling. She helped me get half way up and the rest I did myself. Once I got up I took baby steps then I started to walk, then I trotted, cantered, and finally I galloped.

My mother was very surprised when I galloped. She knew I had the strength and heart of my father who was a wild white stallion and leader of the herd.

Spring is a beautiful season since there are so many kinds of flowers that bloom. Mother says that there are four seasons during the year. There are spring, summer, fall, and winter. Mother also says that I was born in the spring like the other foals in the herd.

Summer followed spring which is beautiful and a much hotter season. The reason it's hot is because of the sun which is stronger during the summer. It makes the green grass warm too. The herd and I gallop through the green plain and we see flowers in different colors. The trees are greener than ever in this season as well.

I always love to gallop on the green plain with the other foals in the sun. It's nice to see other wild animals playing around. We always seem to feel free with no worries to make us feel frightened. That's because of my father since he protects the herd from any dangers.

During the summer I met up with another foal named Shadow. Oh, I'm Crystal by the way. Sorry I forgot to introduce myself. Shadow looks like me and is a darker color than I am.

We became good friends and soon I met his mother. My mother and Shadow's mother were talking, and I overheard them say Shadow and his mother had no herd to be with. My mother told Shadow's mother that they could stay with us and be a part of our herd.

Shadow told me that he never liked to stay in a herd because he liked to see different lands. We made a deal that he could come and go when he wanted to, and to visit me when he returned.

Fall came after the summer. The leaves on the trees changed into beautiful colors. The colors were red, yellow, orange, brown, and purple. After the leaves changed colors, they began to fall off the trees. They turned the green plain into a beautiful, colorful field. The other foals and I loved to jump into the colorful leaves on the ground and simply have fun.

Winter followed after fall and with it came snow. It was the first time I saw snow. It looked like a white blanket that covered the green plain, and the trees. My mother told me that when it gets cold enough the rain turns into snow, which was frozen water. In winter we traveled to different places to find food, water, shelter, and to stay warm. It was fun to play in the snow with the other foals and not have the flies we had in the summer to make us itch.

* * *

A few years passed and I turned four years old. That's when I became a full grown adult. After I turned four, my mother gave me the job of helping the herd.

An average day is always hard. Some mares that are pregnant need help and I comfort them so they can give birth. I see the foals grow and get stronger. It's very comforting to see the herd grow larger and have fun with no worries.

One day while I was watching the foals I saw a white horse galloping on the green plain. He was coming toward my herd. Then I realized that it was Shadow. I had not seen him for a long time. I started galloping to meet him.

We greeted each other and I told him how I took over mother's job of helping the herd. I also told him how many foals were born over the years. Shadow told me that he would stay and help me and the herd because he met other male horses. They advised Shadow that it's better to be in a herd than by himself which is much harder to live than being with a herd.

A few days passed and a beautiful warm spring day arrived. While I was watching the foals, I saw a chestnut colored horse walking in the distance. There was something strange about the horse. It had something on its' back. It was nothing I had ever seen before and the herd was frightened.

It was a strange creature that stood on its hind legs and could walk on them. The creature was sitting on some strange item that was on top of the horse's back. We didn't trust the creature, so Shadow and my father moved the herd away for safety.

I stayed with Shadow. When the creature got off the horse to go to the river and get water, I went to the horse. I talked to her and asked what the creature was. The horse's name was Sunshine and she told me that the creature was called a human.

When the human and Sunshine left, I went to the herd and told them what Sunshine had said. The herd was confused and we all wondered why Sunshine and the human came to our beautiful green plain. Why had they gone back in the same direction as they had come from? Was there something the strange human wanted to find? I guess some questions can't be answered yet.

A few days later Shadow announced that he was going to leave the herd again. He said he thought about the human and wondered if there were other lands out there he had not seen.

Just before Shadow was going to leave we saw another herd of horses with a human on each of their backs galloping toward us. There was something strange about how they were acting and my mother and father moved the herd away for safety.

Shadow and I would distract the humans so the herd could get away. Soon the humans started chasing us and caught us with something that was called a rope. Soon after, my adventure began.

Chapter 2

"Where are the humans taking us?" I asked, but the horses looked a little frightened.

"I heard the humans say that they are going to break you," one of the horses told us. That means they are going to break our spirits of being wild.

A few days and nights passed, and then finally we came upon a wide open space with something that one of the horses called a ranch. The humans were nice and let Shadow, me, and the other horses rest for the day and night with other horses. Shadow and I became friends with the other horses.

"Why do the humans want to break us?" I asked the other horses.

Suddenly, Shadow and I saw Sunshine walking towered us.

She said, "The human that rode on me told the other humans that he saw you with your herd on the green plain."

Shadow and I finally understood why Sunshine and the human went to our beautiful green plain. They needed more horses for some reason, and found us.

The next morning one of the humans took Shadow to get broken. The other horses had told us that with constant and slow work, the humans try to gain our trust by letting them saddle us and ride us. This has been going on for a long time now and the other horses don't know why.

Out of nowhere, a much smaller human came up to us and asked with a big smile on her face, "May I ride the Stallion?"

The other humans looked frightened. The smaller human girl was called Dana by the other humans. Dana has long light brown hair, dark brown eyes, and was wearing light blue clothes as the day time sky.

There was also another human girl just as tall as Dana. The humans called her Rachel. She has long black hair, eyes as dark as her hair, and was wearing black clothes as the night time sky.

Dana is a brave and smart girl who is not afraid of what she wants to do. Rachel is a smart girl like Dana, but calmer and easy going. Rachel helps Dana calm down when she loses her temper, but both girls are nice and are best of friends.

"Why are you staring at me like that?" Dana asked with a light but strong voice. "Can I ride the white Stallion?"

"No," answered a human called Robert in a stern voice. Robert is taller than Dana and he has short brown hair, dark brown eyes like hers, and was wearing brown clothes. "You can't ride the white Stallion. It's too wild!"

"But, father…"

"Oh, will you calm down Dana," Rachel interrupted. "You can't always fight with your father just because he doesn't let you ride the horses that he catches every day!"

When Dana said "father", I jumped in amazement. They look similar, but act very differently.

"Dana's father runs the ranch," Sunshine told me. "He always tells Dana to not ride any of the horses until after they are broken and well tamed."

"Rachel, don't tell me what to do," Dana said sternly. "I'm fine. I just don't want my father to get more wild horses to break."

"I know," Rachel quickly answered. "You tell me that all the time, and I get sick of hearing it."

While Robert was trying to saddle Shadow, in which Shadow did not like it and would run away every chance he got in the round pen, Dana thought for a while.

Suddenly Dana snapped her fingers together and with a grin on her face turned to Rachel.

"I've got an idea," Dana whispered to Rachel so her father would not hear her. "Why don't we let the horses go free, to return to their herds?"

"Are you crazy?" Rachel whispered back. "Your father will be very mad at you, and how can you do that? The whole ranch is filled with people."

When Rachel said that, Dana looked puzzled.

She never thought of how to get us free. She thought for another moment. Then, she looked like she had another idea.

"At night," Dana whispered excitedly. "It might be the only way to get the white horses out. They're the only horses on the ranch that are not broken. It might…"

"Dana," yelled Rachel in a whisper. "You have to calm down and don't worry; I will help you all the way."

"You will?" Dana asked with a grin and hugged Rachel. "Thank you so much Rachel; I'm glad I have a friend like you that will always help me when I need it."

"You're welcome," Rachel answered.

That night, Dana and Rachel went outside to get us out of the ranch. Dana led me and Rachel led Shadow out with ropes on us, but Shadow and I didn't like the ropes. Dana and Rachel walked us as far as they could and stopped near a stream to remove the ropes.

"There," they said at the same time as if to be in harmony. "You're free."

When we left, we had no idea that Dana and Rachel were in trouble. A friend of Dana's father called Ricky had followed us with his own mysterious plans. He looks like Dana's father, but has light brown eyes and wrinkles under his eyes and neck.

Dana and Rachel screamed when Ricky grabbed them and they tried to break free.

I heard Ricky say in a low voice, "I finally caught you two. Now all I have to do is get Richard to step down from his position and I can take over."

Before he could carry them away, Rachel bit Ricky's hand and Dana did the same.

When Ricky let go with pain, they ran. Shadow and I heard Dana and Rachel scream, and saw that they were running toward us.

Then we saw Ricky running after them yelling with anger, "Get back here."

When Dana and Rachel got closer to us, I suggested to Shadow that I thought we should wait for them. I reminded Shadow that the girls had helped us to escape and Shadow agreed.

"We should still be careful though, since they're humans," said Shadow.

"I know," I answered with a calm voice. "I will be careful around them."

Dana and Rachel looked at us with puzzled faces wondering why we were standing still, and not running away.

"Why do you think they are standing there?" Dana asked Rachel in huffing breaths. "They should be running."

"I don't know," Rachel answered with a low voice. "This might sound crazy, but I think they want to help us."

"I was thinking the same thing," Dana agreed. "It might be for helping them get out of the ranch."

When Dana and Rachel caught up with us, we let them sit on our backs. Rachel was on Shadow and Dana was on me. Shadow and I started to gallop as fast as we could, away from Ricky to get the girls to safety.

Chapter 3

We galloped far away from the ranch and Ricky, until it started to rain and clouds took over the sky making it dark.

"We need to find shelter," Dana yelled as loud as she could to Rachel so she could hear over the thunder. "It's getting worse out here."

"I know," yelled Rachel as loud as she could like Dana. "Where can we go?"

"In here ladies," said an old man in a dirty shelter that almost blended in with the landscape and was in the middle of a forest. "Come in my house and get out of the rain, and you can put the horses in the stable."

"It might be the only way," Dana yelled puzzled. "At least for the night, so the horses can dry off and rest."

So, Shadow and I walked into what the old man called a stable. We didn't trust the old man because he was another human, but at least we could get out of the rain.

Once inside, the girls dried Shadow and me off and put us in an enclosure which had food and water.

"Thank you," Dana said to the old man as they all were walking into his house.

Inside the house, the humans talked:

"Who are you?" Dana asked.

"I am David," he answered while they sat down on the couches. David is an old man with short gray curly hair, has light green eyes, and was wearing camo color clothes. "Who are you ladies?"

"Sorry, we never introduced ourselves," Dana said. "I'm Dana and this is my friend Rachel. It's nice to meet you."

"Where did you come from?" David asked.

"We came from my father's ranch," Dana answered calmly. "His friend, Ricky, grabbed us when we were trying to do something."

"Dana," Rachel said in a low voice. "I don't know if we should tell him anything."

"It's alright," David said to Rachel firmly. "I am a retired soldier from the army and I would like to help."

"You're a retired soldier?" Dana and Rachel asked together at the same time looking at each other with their mouths open.

"So," David said laughing. "Now, will you tell me how I can help?"

"It started like this," Dana said with a deep breath. "My father collects wild horses and tries to break every one of them to control the population, but he's taking them away from their families and homes."

"So, Dana had an idea," Rachel said taking a turn. "The idea was that we should help the only two horses on the ranch that were not broken."

"That's when we came to the river," Dana said having another turn. "We let the two white stallions go free, but we never knew that we were being followed by a ranch hand my father recently hired named Ricky.

"That's when he grabbed us," Rachel said for her turn. "He said he finally caught us and could get Dana's father to step down from his job. We were able to get away from Ricky with the help of the two horses and now we're here."

"Sounds like an adventure," David said with enthusiasm and understanding. "Now, you two girls should take the two white stallions back to their families, if you know where they live."

"We don't," Rachel said with a sad expression.

"My father never tells me or Rachel where he finds the wild horses." Dana said.

"Hmm, maybe the white horses know how to get home," David said.

"If we let the horses go, then what about Ricky?" Dana asked troubled. "He might want to catch them and show my father."

"We have to be careful," David answered nodding. "I will try to help by finding Ricky, but until then, you two girls should stay here. Also, don't be so mad at your father. It may be hard to understand now, but his job is important."

David went out to find Ricky.

Back in the stable:

When the storm was over Shadow and I started to wonder how long we were going to be in the stable.

"I want to get out of here," I said with anger kicking the wall. "I'm a wild horse!"

"Calm down, Crystal," Shadow said in a soft voice. "The humans will let us out and we will be free again."

"I hope your right," I answered in a calmer voice. Then, I spotted David running out of the house. "Where's the old man going, and what's wrong?"

"I don't know," Shadow answered in a confused voice.

Back in the house, a few hours passed by:

"Hey Rachel, I think we should help David," Dana suggested. "I mean, what if he gets hurt?"

"David will be fine," Rachel answered with a grin. "Although it would not hurt to make sure David will be fine."

"Awesome," Dana yelled with a smile on her face. "Let's go."

Dana and Rachel came to our stable and asked, "can both of you help us?"

"We're going to follow David and we might need your help." Dana asked with a bright smile.

Shadow and I thought about it for a few seconds and then nodded our heads.

They got on our backs and we started to gallop to see what would lie ahead.

"This trip we're going on is a little strange," Dana said to herself thinking hard. "I feel like I know this, but differently."

"Why is that, Dana?" Rachel asked confused. "I don't understand."

"I read this book," Dana answered with a deep breath. "It was about two girls who had horses and they had an adventure, like we are now, but things happened. Bad things, but I think it's all in my head."

"That's weird," Rachel answered. "What's the name of the book?"

"I think it was called, Trip to Albemore," Dana answered still thinking hard. "It was a good book, but it's the same, as if we were actually in the book."

While Dana, Rachel, Shadow, and I were trying to catch up with David, something happened that would change everything.

Up ahead, David looked for clues to find Ricky, but he never knew Ricky was watching him the whole time. When David wasn't looking, Ricky came up behind David, hit him on the head with a rock, and knocked him out. Ricky put David on his tall, black horse, and rode into the distance.

A piece of paper fell out of Ricky's bag while he ran away.

Dana, Rachel, Shadow, and I came galloping to where David was captured, but we never knew that anything had happened to our new friend.

"I thought we would catch up with David by now," Dana said confused. "He was supposed to be here, I think."

"We can find him later," Rachel answered confidently. "Right now, I think we should rest because the horses are tired from running."

"Maybe, we should name them," Dana said. "They have names, but I just wish we knew what they were."

"Let's make up names," Rachel answered. "I think I'll call the horse I'm riding on, Ghost, because in the rain he looked like he was shining in the light of the moon."

"I don't know what to call mine," Dana said thinking. "I will call her, Angel, because she was always nice and gentle when I rode her."

Shadow and I thought those were good names for us, so we let Dana and Rachel call us by these human names.

"Hey Rachel, come look at what I have found," Dana yelled to Rachel.

Dana had been looking for any signs or clues of David in case he was hurt.

"Look, I found David's hat."

"It must be Ricky!" Rachel shouted in an angry voice. "I don't trust that man."

"We have to find him," Dana said worried. "He might have hurt David."

"Hey, look," Rachel said calming down. "Ricky might have dropped this map. It shows us where he was going and it might be where he's hiding. So let's find him and save our friend."

Chapter 4

As night turned to day, Dana and Rachel got on our backs to go find David. We all knew it would be a long journey, so we went back to David's cabin to stock up on supplies.

"What's first on the map, Rachel?" Dana asked once we headed out. "Ricky might be anywhere on the map."

"It looks like a desert," Rachel answered puzzled looking at the map while riding Shadow. "I think there's also a different part, like a rain forest and an ocean."

"Ricky does know where to hide," Dana joked. "He goes far away so no one can find him."

"But, that means it will be harder to find him," Rachel said making a point. "Even if we get past all of this, he might be anywhere around those parts on the map that we can't get to."

While Dana, Rachel, Shadow, and I were looking for Ricky and David; Ricky was hiding at an underground dark brown warehouse. It had two broken windows that had different equipment inside it.

"What are you planning to do, Ricky?" David asked from within in his cell. "What are you going to do with the girls?"

"First," Ricky answered. "Since your never getting out of here, I'll tell you my plan. Day and night I have to work for that devil, Robert, and listen to his commands telling me what to do. All he does is order me around, but he never lets me lead. At night I do all his dirty work by washing the horses and feeding them the next morning with just a little sleep. So, I thought of a plan. If I try to get to his daughter and act as though to hurt her, he will give in. I will take over the ranch and make Robert work for me."

"So, you only care about yourself and your feelings," David said with anger. "Why don't you just ask Robert to be nicer instead of keeping me here? Why do you want to keep me here anyway?"

"I know that you will try to get to Robert, and tell him my plan," Ricky snarled. "I will be able to use you and the girls as bait to get at Robert. I know the girls are coming to save you. I have left a map behind for them to follow so that they will find us here."

David looked at Robert in horror, "That fool, Robert, doesn't know my real plan yet, but he will soon find out," Ricky said to himself with an evil smile.

Meanwhile out in the desert, "It's so hot," Dana said tired. "Can I have water?"

"Alright, but don't drink too much," Rachel answered as tired as Dana is. "Give some to the horses as well; they're getting tired too. Man, we have to get out of this sun."

"Agreed," Dana answered.

"How far do you think this desert is, Rachel?" Dana asked giving us water. "I don't think the horses can take much more of this. We ride on them, so they have to be more tired than us."

"I don't know, Dana," Rachel answered. "I think we should hurry. It feels like it's getting hotter."

"I know," Dana said walking to where Rachel was looking out further into the desert. "It does, and do you feel a strong breeze?"

"I do," Rachel answered with a confused face. "It feels like…"

Then, Rachel and Dana saw what it was and yelled at the same time, "SAND STORM!"

"Run Angel and Ghost, Run!" Dana yelled to Shadow and me, but we waited for Dana and Rachel until they got on our backs.

"Hurry, we need to find shelter and fast!" yelled Dana.

We galloped as fast as we could with the girls on our backs.

"Hey, is that shelter?" Dana asked trying to look through the dust.

"It looks like it, so let's go Ghost," Rachel yelled.

Shadow and I entered a shelter that had no roof on top of it. There was no door and the inside was like a maze. We hid in one of the maze's paths until the sand storm ended.

"I'm glad that sand storm is over." Rachel said in relief. "The sand made us lose our way, and I don't know where we are."

"I don't know where we are either," Dana answered puzzled trying to get the sand out of her hair. "It looks like Angel and Ghost are fine, but it was odd that the sand storm came when we were off the horses."

"I think it was just coincidence since sand storms happen all the time in the dessert," Rachel said.

While we were on the long journey to find Ricky and David; back at the ranch, Robert was worried about Dana and Rachel.

"I've been looking everywhere for Dana and Rachel," Robert said angrily. "Has anyone found those white horses?"

"Sir, we found a note," said one of Robert's men.

"Thank you; now go back to finding the white horses with the others. Now, what did Dana write?" Robert asked himself:

"Dear father, Rachel and I took the white horses to free them. I don't care if you're mad because this makes me happy. You have to stop catching wild horses to break. I hope you still love me, but I have to do this. You always said that what you should do is follow your heart, and I am doing just that. I'm going to follow my heart. I love you, and I will try to come home as soon as I can."

Love,
Dana

"Why didn't she tell me how she felt?" Robert asked himself. "Men, we have to find Dana and Rachel. I just hope they're alright."

Dana, Rachel, Shadow, and I were all walking across the desert, hoping we would get out of it soon. We found our way back on track after the sand storm blew away.

"How much farther is this desert?" Dana asked angrily. "I'm so tired from this heat, and I know you are too."

"Calm down Dana," Rachel answered until we heard a sound that was: AROO-OO-OO.

"What was that?" Rachel asked with a scared voice.

"I think that was a coyote," Dana answered nervously. "I think I can also see it."

The coyote was on top of a high rocky ledge, and started to jump down from ledge to ledge getting closer to us. When the coyote reached the bottom, Dana said calmly, "It looks hungry. Maybe if I give it some food it will go away."

"No Dana, you are not giving it any of our food." Rachel answered in a strict voice. "If you give this coyote any of our food it will follow us like a regular dog, and I don't want that."

"It might become our friend," Dana said trying to convince Rachel. "Blackie might help us find Ricky and David."

"Oh, so now you're calling it, 'Blackie?'" Rachel asked. "Is it because of its black fur, or do you want a wild animal following us?"

"Come on, it might be fun helping a coyote," Dana said still trying to convince Rachel. "Blackie might help us with sniffing around."

"Fine," Rachel answered in annoyance. "Just be careful on how much you feed it."

"I'll be fine, Rachel," Dana said anxiously as she was getting closer to the coyote. "Here boy, come here Blackie."

The black coyote looked at Dana when she called him a name, but it still growled at her. When "Blackie," saw the food Dana was going to give to him, he stopped growling.

"Blackie stopped growling," Rachel said to herself in amazement. "When did I start calling the coyote, Blackie? Ugh, Dana was right. He was hungry, and I think he's happy now."

"See, I told you," Dana said rubbing it in while getting closer to the coyote. "Here Blackie, come here boy."

The black coyote started to walk up to Dana, and then he took the food from her hand. Blackie let Dana pet him.

"Wow," said Dana surprised, petting the coyote. "Hello Blackie."

The black coyote looked at Dana when he was done eating and started to lick her face. Dana fell in love with him instantly.

"Blackie, meet your new friends," Dana said having one hand out showing Blackie who his new friends were. "That's Rachel in the black clothes, and the two white horses are Angel and Ghost."

After making friends with Blackie, we continued to walk across the desert, but it was still very hot.

"What's after the desert, Rachel?" Dana asked tired. "I hope it's cooler than this sun?"

"I think the map has a rain forest," Rachel answered. "I think we might be there."

We all looked in amazement until Dana, Rachel, and Blackie started to run toward it. Then Shadow and I started to run into the shady forest.

"Finally some shade, but that's very odd that a rain forest is connected to a desert," Dana said confused. "I'm not complaining, but I hope we find David and Ricky soon."

"Well first, let's get some rest," Rachel said. "I'm tired and I can't move my legs. Besides, we can't find David and save him if we're tired."

"Your right, Rachel," Dana answered. "How does that sound, Blackie?"

When Dana looked at Blackie, he was already asleep under the shade of the trees, which made him blend in with the surrounding area. Blackie sometimes snored when he was asleep, and every time he snored, Dana and Rachel giggled. They tried to giggle in a soft voice, but it was hard not to laugh at him.

After Dana and Rachel stopped giggling at Blackie, we all took his idea and rested as long as we could.

After a couple of hours, Blackie finally woke up to see Dana awake as well, and staring into the deepness of the forest. I was awake, but I didn't want to disturb Dana and Blackie since they were very close to each other.

Blackie walked up to Dana and sat next to her looking into the forest as she did, but was worried about her and kept looking up at her. Finally, Dana realized Blackie was next to her and said to him, "Oh, good afternoon sleepyhead. Did you have a good sleep?" Blackie nodded, but Dana knew he was worried about her.

"Don't worry, Blackie," Dana said looking at him and petting him. "I'm fine; I just couldn't get back to sleep. Did you know you snore in your sleep?"

Blackie looked away as if to be embarrassed and Dana giggled, but looked back into the forest.

"I'm up because I was confused," Dana said to Blackie looking into the forest. "I was confused on how much that desert was so similar to a book I once read. That's why I couldn't get back to sleep."

After they sat for a bit in silence, Dana stood up.

"We should start moving, it's been a while and we need to save David." Dana and Blackie woke us all up and we continued on through the forest.

Chapter 5

"I love nature, I just feel at home," Dana said laughing. "I also love to see all the wild animals that live here, and to be with friends too."

"Why are you laughing?" Rachel asked as if to be annoyed.

"I just feel happy for some reason," Dana answered continuing to laugh. "Why? Do you want me to stop?"

"No, I'm just wondering," Rachel answered. "You want to guess how deep this rain forest is?"

"No, but I do think it's going to take as long to travel through as it did in the desert," Dana answered. "I bet the ocean's going to be just as long too, and I wonder if there are any traps. I wonder if there's something that's going to happen while we're here like the sand storm in the desert."

"Maybe, and I think you're right," Rachel said wondering.

"Right about what, Rachel?" Dana asked confused. "I don't get it."

"Right about, Ricky," Rachel answered. "I think he will have traps for us and maybe he sent Blackie too."

"Well, if he did, that plan failed," Dana said petting Blackie. "Isn't that right boy?"

Blackie nodded and let Dana pet him, but Rachel was worried. I knew that Dana felt worried as well. All of us were feeling uneasy about the whole thing.

While we were in the rain forest, Ricky was furious:

"How could they have survived?" Ricky yelled angrily smashing the equipment. "I spent much of my time working on the perfect route for them to follow and get caught in that sand storm. I even sent that dumb coyote."

"Maybe you should just give up," David said still locked up in the cell. "You can't win, and the girls will stop you. I'm sure of that."

"Well, let's see how good they are with the other traps I made for them," Ricky said with a grin on his face. "They won't be able to take this trip much longer."

David was still worried that Ricky might be right, but he somehow knew the girls would get through it.

Back at the ranch:

Everyone was getting their horses ready to find us.

"Where do we start looking first, sir?" one of Robert's men asked.

"I think I know," Robert answered to himself. "I think it's by the stream Dana and I used to go to."

"Excuse me sir?" another one of Robert's men asked confused.

"By the stream," Robert yelled. "Everyone follow me."

They all started to follow Robert on their horses hoping to find us.

In the forest, several hours had past of just walking through the trees:

Dana and Rachel were walking with us and Blackie instead of riding us.

"It's getting darker out," Rachel said. "I think we should make camp for the night."

"I think so too," Dana agreed with Rachel.

"It's so dark that I can't see Blackie. Wait, where's Blackie?" Dana got so scared that she started to call Blackie's name, but didn't know he was beside her the whole time.

"Wait, what's beside me?" Dana asked petting Blackie, but didn't know. "Oh, it's you Blackie. Try not to scare me next time. I thought I lost you."

The next morning, we started to walk through the rain forest while Dana and Rachel were riding us with Blackie following close by.

"What tricks do you think Ricky has for us, Rachel?" Dana asked. "Why does he want to do this?"

"I don't know, Dana," Rachel answered. "I know it's something bad."

"It just struck me," Dana said with a worried face. "I wonder if my father knows that we're gone."

"Maybe he found your letter," Rachel added. "He might be coming to find us."

"I hope not," Dana said with a worried face. "I don't want my father to go through what we had to. He might get hurt."

"I'm sure your father's fine, Dana," Rachel answered trying to calm her down. "He's very strong, and you know that nothing will stop him from achieving his goal."

"You got that right," Dana said calming down. "What if Ricky find's him, and tries to do something worse."

"Dana calm down!" Rachel commanded. "Your father is fine, and Ricky wouldn't dare hurt him."

"When I find Ricky," Dana said with an angry face. "He's going to be sorry even if he didn't hurt my father. He took David and that's enough for me. He tried to grab us too, so I'm really mad right now."

"But one thing I want to know is why Ricky is doing this?" Dana asked with an angry face. "I mean, does he have a grudge against me? Does he hate my father for some reason? What?"

"If you ask me, I think he hates both you and your father," Rachel answered.

"Why do you think that, Rachel?" Dana asked confused.

"Well, think of Ricky for a second," Rachel answered. "He might hate you for being rich or having your own land. He has been jealous of your family for a while now, I've noticed."

"You know, Rachel," Dana said. "I think you're right. I've seen it too, and he has been acting weird for a couple of months now. But my father hasn't been noticing anything because he's been so busy."

"How about we stop thinking about Ricky for a while," Rachel suggested. "Let's give the horses a break; so how about we walk with them and get some exercise."

The girls got off us, and started to walk with us. Blackie liked to have Dana walking with him. After walking for many miles, Dana said, "Rachel, we've been walking for hours. How close are we getting to the end of this rain forest, or near the ocean?"

"I don't know," Rachel answered. "We might have taken a wrong turn, or something."

"Or, maybe we're lost," Dana said making a point. "Like you said, we might have taken a wrong turn somewhere, or we are going the right way since all the trees look the same."

"I just hope this won't take too long," Rachel added.

Both the girl's stopped walking and stared at something which was glowing, but no one knew what it was.

First, Shadow and I saw little wings flapping, and then we started to see that it was a little white Pegasus. It had blue wings, and a black mane and tail.

"Wow," Dana and Rachel said at the same time. "It's a mini Pegasus."

The Pegasus, whose name was Whisper, came to Shadow and me. We talked to her for a while, but Dana and Rachel looked confused. The girls looked as if they could not believe what they were seeing.

"What do you think that Angel, Ghost, and the Pegasus are talking about?" Dana asked leaning close to Rachel.

"Maybe they're talking about being friends, or about our journey," Rachel answered.

When Shadow, Whisper, and I were done talking to each other, we went over to Dana, Rachel, and Blackie to introduce Whisper.

"Hi," Dana said holding Whisper in her hand.

"She looks beautiful," Rachel said looking at her.

"My name is Whisper; it's nice to meet you."

The girls were surprised when Whisper could talk to them.

"How can you talk?" Dana asked. "I thought that Pegasus's were taller than what you are."

"Somehow, a spell was cast upon me that keeps me small," Whisper answered. "For some reason I can talk, but I think it's from the spell. The white horses you are riding are named Crystal and Shadow. I thought you should know."

Chapter 6

"So, the white horse I'm riding is, Crystal?" Dana asked. "The horse Rachel is riding is called, Shadow."

"I still think that Ghost and Angel were good names," Rachel said. "Can we still call them those names or should we call them by their real names?"

"Why don't you ask them yourselves?" Whisper said while she was flying over to Shadow and me. Then, she put dust on us. I sneezed and shivered feeling a tingling over my body. Shadow did the same.

"Why did you put that dust on us, Whisper?" I asked. "I feel really different now."

The girls gasped and looked at me as if they understood me. Then, they said at the same time, "You can talk!"

"She can?" Shadow asked confused. "How can she talk?"

"You can talk too, Ghost," Rachel said in amazement. "I mean, Shadow."

"Wait, I'm confused," Dana said holding her head. "What did you do to them, Whisper?"

"Even though I have a spell on me," Whisper said. "I'm still a Pegasus, and Pegasus' have powers. So I gave Crystal and Shadow the power to talk to you girls."

"Thank you," Shadow and I said at the same time like Dana and Rachel did.

"You girls can call us what you want." Shadow said looking down at them.

"I think we will go with your real names," Dana said. "I would want someone to call me by my real name."

"I agree," Rachel said nodding her head.

"What about Blackie? Can you do the same to him, Whisper?" Dana asked with excitement.

"You mean the black coyote?" Whisper asked puzzled. "I can give him the power to talk as well."

Whisper went over to Blackie, and put dust over him like she did to Shadow and me. Blackie didn't move or do anything until Whisper stopped putting the dust on him. He shook the extra dust off and sat down again.

"Thank you, Whisper," Blackie said in a deep voice. "Hello, Dana, Rachel, Crystal, and Shadow; it's good to talk to you. My name is Jack by the way."

"Thank you, Whisper," Dana said. "There's one more question I would like to ask you. I would like to ask if you could help us find our friend, David. He was kidnapped by this man who used to be my father's helper at his ranch, named Ricky."

"I would love to help," Whisper answered. "Where do we have to go?"

"We follow this map," Rachel answered. "This house is where David and Ricky are."

"Good," Dana said eagerly. "Now, we have Whisper to help us and she can fly. We can know how far away from the ocean we are."

"I'm glad to help," Whisper said. "The ocean is not far away from where we're standing."

"It's not, that's great!" Dana yelled with glee.

"What I mean is, this is a large rain forest," Whisper answered. "I've been here for many years, and I know where the ocean is. We should be there by tomorrow."

"Now, I think we should start walking so we can get to the ocean faster," Dana said.

"Whisper can show us the way," Rachel continued. "I just hope we're not too late."

"Well, let's just start going," Jack suggested. "We can cover more ground, and get to the ocean quicker."

"Ok, smart dog," Rachel said making a joke. "We'll go."

"Very funny, Rachel," Jack said while Dana was giggling. "I mean it. We have to hurry, so we can save David."

"Jack's right, Rachel," Dana said calming down. "We do have to hurry. We don't know what Ricky will do to him."

"Alright, alright, will you both just calm down?" Rachel asked a little angry. "Now Whisper, can you show us the way since Mr. and Mrs. Impatient can't wait any longer."

"Hey," Lynn and Jack said at the same time. "We are not impatient."

"I know, I'm just joking with you two," Rachel said giggling. "So, let's get going."

"Very funny Rachel," Dana said.

We all started to walk and follow Whisper, but Shadow and I were still worried about what might happen ahead. We walked until nightfall, and we were all tired from walking for hours.

"We should stop for the night," Dana said. "We need all of our energy to finish getting through the rain forest and to the ocean."

"Dana's right," Rachel agreed. "We should all rest for the night."

"We will get to the ocean tomorrow," Whisper said. "It's not too far now, and we can go in the morning."

During the night Shadow, Jack, Whisper, and I heard something in the bushes, but we didn't know what it was.

"Dana, Rachel, get up," I whispered. "Something's watching us."

"What, what's wrong?" Dana asked trying to open her eyes.

Rachel tried to do the same thing next to her.

"What's that noise?" Rachel asked. "It sounds like a dog or something in the bushes."

"I don't think that's a dog in the bushes," I said. "I think it's a wolf."

Suddenly, three wolves jumped out of the bushes surrounding us and growling. Jack went to the wolf that was Alpha. That means it's the head wolf that the other wolves listen to. Jack tried to talk to it. We all watched. Jack talked to the Alpha in wolf tongue, but it didn't look like the Alpha wanted to talk to Jack.

"What's the wolf saying?" Dana asked Jack. "What are you saying to him?"

"He said that he wants to eat us because we are in his territory," Jack answered. "I'm trying to tell him that he can't."

Jack talked to the wolves again, but they didn't want to listen any more. So, the Alpha bit Jack on his back, picked him up, and threw him off to the side. Jack yelped in pain when the Alpha did that.

"Jack," Dana yelled concerned.

We backed away while the Alpha was walking toward us slowly, until Jack jumped in front of us and started to growl at the wolves. Two of the wolves went in back of us, but Jack was going to fight with the Alpha wolf.

Jack took the first move by jumping on the Alpha, starting the fight. We had to take care of the other two wolves. One of the two wolves jumped toward me, but I kicked the wolf in the air. Then, the other wolf went to Shadow, but Shadow did the same thing that I did.

Both the wolves tried to repeat the same thing they did after they fell to the ground, but Shadow and I did the same thing as we did before keeping them from attacking the girls.

Just then, Whisper went to the two wolves and hit them in the eyes with her dust. The wolves closed their eyes, shook their heads, and tried to rub themselves with their paws. Then, Shadow and I trotted up to them and pushed them over. Both the wolves ran away yelping.

Jack and the Alpha were still fighting. Jack bit the Alpha's leg and the Alpha yelped. Then, the Alpha grabbed Jack's tail and he yelped. Then, the Alpha threw Jack into the bushes and we couldn't see Jack.

Shadow and I had enough of the fighting, so we pushed the Alpha when he wasn't looking. Then, the Alpha jumped, but Shadow kicked him and when the Alpha fell to the ground he ran. Shadow ran after him a little until he was out of his sight. Then, Shadow walked back to where we were.

"Jack," Dana yelled running to where he was lying down. "Jack, Jack; are you alright?"

"I'm fine, Dana," Jack said looking at her and trying to get up. "I'm just…ouch, that hurts."

"You should stay there," Dana said. "You have too many wounds. Rachel do you still have that first aid kit?"

"Right here," Rachel answered giving it to Dana. "Just don't use all of it."

"I won't," Dana answered. "Thanks. Now, let me see your wounds, but first I need to wash that blood off of you. Then I can try and bandage you."

Shadow and I took some buckets to get some water from a spring that Whisper showed us. Holding the buckets in our mouths to fill up by the stream and then headed back to where the other were. Dana poured some water on Jack where his wounds were to get the extra blood off of his fur.

"That sting's," Jack said hissing with pain. "Can you do that slower?"

"Sorry, but it will sting a while," Dana answered. "Now, let me just bandage you up and you should heal up in no time."

"Thank you, Dana," Jack said. "Now, we should start moving so we can get to the ocean."

"No we're not," Dana said sounding like a mother worried about her child. "We're going to rest until the sun comes up. Until then, you're going to stay there for the rest of the night so you can get your energy back."

"Alright," Jack agreed resting his head in Dana's lap.

Chapter 7

The next morning we started to walk toward the ocean while Whisper was leading us. After a few hours, we began to smell the salt water from the ocean.

"Here we are," Whisper said. "We're right at the ocean."

"Wow," Dana and Rachel said at the same time.

"Yes, it is beautiful," Jack agreed walking slowly. "We don't have much time though. We have to find something that will carry us across the ocean."

"Jack's right," Shadow said until he saw something. "What is that?"

"I don't know," I answered looking at it, and then everyone looked in the same direction.

"It looks like a passenger ship that's been deserted for a while," Dana answered surprised.

"Your right, Dana," Rachel agreed. "It is a passenger ship, but I wonder why it's here?"

"Me too," Dana answered. "What I wonder about is if it still runs."

"Dana's right," Jack said. "If it does run, we might be able to use it to cross the ocean to where David and Ricky are."

"Well, what are we waiting for," Dana said. "Let's see if it works so we can get away from this rain forest."

"Then, let's go," Rachel agreed. "I also want to get away from this rain forest."

We started to walk toward the passenger ship, but we didn't know that there were people on it, and that they worked for Ricky.

"How do we get in?" I asked. "Shadow, Jack, and I can't climb in."

"I don't know," Dana answered. "We'll find a way in."

"That might not be a problem," Rachel said. "There's a way in through the back."

"That's convenient?" Dana said. "I thought it would be locked."

"It should be," Rachel agreed looking confused. "I guess something happened."

Dana looked as confused as Rachel while tapping her mouth. "Or, maybe someone is still running it."

"Maybe," Rachel said. "I just don't know what else to use around here that will take us across the ocean."

"We'll use it," Rachel answered.

Then Dana asked in a loud voice, "What?"

Then Rachel said, "Calm down Dana. We'll use it only if no one else is using it. If there are people in it, then, we'll see if they can help us."

"Let's do it," Jack said. "It will be the only way to cross the ocean with or without anyone using it."

"Ok, then let's do it," Dana said. "Just in case, let's be careful."

We all started to walk into the passenger ship, and we started to look around for people. We didn't meet anyone until we went to the top of the ship which is called the deck. We never saw anyone on the deck, so we started to think no one was using it.

Until, we went to where the captain steers the ship. Many people were there, and we thought the whole crew was there which looked like a meeting.

Everyone was in chairs talking until Dana and Rachel walked into the captain's room. Shadow, Jack, Whisper, and I weren't there because Shadow and I couldn't fit. Jack and Whisper stayed behind because Dana and Rachel didn't want to scare anyone.

"Oh, sorry," Dana said while everyone was looking at her and Rachel. "We didn't think anyone was here."

"Oh, well hello girls," the captain said. "Why are you here?"

"Well, we don't have too much time," Rachel answered him. "We're trying to find a friend that might be in trouble, and we need to cross this ocean to save him. Can you help us, please?"

"I would love to help you two girls," the captain answered. "I just need a location as to where we are going." The captain had a dark sailor suite, was big with a bushy mustache.

"We're following this map," Dana said putting down the map on the table. "Do you see this building right here? That's our location."

"I see and if you girls are in a hurry we will start departing right away," the captain said. "I would like to keep this map so we can use it if you don't mind?"

"We don't, you can use it," Rachel answered. "If you don't mind, can we have some friends that are helping us come along?"

"You may," the captain said. "Let's start departing."

Lynn and Rachel said at the same time, "Thank you captain."

We started to cross the ocean. We thought it would be safe until we could get to David, and face Ricky.

"I hope we get to David in time," Dana said. "I'm worried about him."

"Me too, Dana," Rachel agreed. "I'm sure that David's fine."

"I'm going to see the captain," Dana said. "Just to ask him how long it will take to get to that building on the map."

"What?" Rachel asked. "We just left."

"I know," Dana answered. "I just want to see."

"To see what, Dana?" Jack asked walking up to her.

"Oh, hi Jack," Dana said surprised. "How are you doing now, since after the fight?"

"Forget about that," Jack answered. "I'm fine, but thank you. How are you?"

"I'm ok, but I was more concerned about you," Dana answered. "Anyway, I just want to see how long it will take us to get to where David and Ricky are."

"I see, but you just saw the Captain," Jack said confused. "You know that it will take a while until we get across the ocean. Why can't you ask him later?"

"I just want to see," Lynn continued. "That's all."

"To see what, Dana?" Whisper asked, while Shadow and I were walking up to her.

"Aaaaggghhhh," a noise Dana made upsettingly. "Will you two tell them for me, please?"

Dana started to walk up to us. Shadow moved to one side and Whisper and I moved to the other side so Dana could pass between us. We watched her for a few seconds until we all turned and looked at Rachel and Jack.

Then I asked, "Did we miss something?" Then we turned again and watched Dana go back to the Captain's room.

"I think she's nervous," Rachel said with a frown on her face. "I also think that Dana feels that this whole mess is her fault."

"It's not her fault, though." I say confused. "It's Ricky's fault. Why would she feel it's her fault?"

"I think because that she didn't tell her father about what was making her nervous in the first place." Rachel answered. "We both knew something was wrong with Ricky, but we never told anyone our concerns because no one would listen to us anyway. Everyone calls us kids and all the adults think they know what's best."

"Still, it's not you or Dana's fault," Jack said trying to comfort Rachel. "No one could know that any of this would happen. Dana should not blame herself and neither should you."

Rachel gave a small smile and pet Jack saying, "Thank you."

Dana walked up the stairs, went to the door where the captain was steering the ship, and knocked on the door.

"Come in," the captain yelled.

"Hello Captain," Dana said after coming into the room and closing the door behind her. "May I ask a question?"

"Sure," the captain answered. "What's your question?"

"I was just wondering how long it will take to where our destination is?" Dana asked. "Oh, I just remembered. We never introduced each other when we first met."

"We never did, did we?" The captain asked. "I'm Captain Bert, and it should take at least two to three days to where we're heading. Now, what is your name?"

"Oh, I'm sorry. My name is Dana and my friend's name is Rachel," Dana answered. "Thank you Captain Bert."

"Wait, you and your friend's names are Dana and Rachel?" Captain Bert asked Dana looking at her with a straight face.

"Yes," Dana answered him confused. "Why, Captain Bert?"

"Then you are in trouble," Captain Bert answered with a grin. "For everyone on this ship except you and your friends work for Ricky."

Chapter 8

Dana gasped and started to run so she could warn the others. Then, Captain Bert rushed after her to grab her, but Dana was too fast and he missed. Dana was able to run out the door and Captain Bert pressed a button that started an alarm system. The alarm was heard throughout the passenger ship, but Rachel, Shadow, Whisper, Jack, and I didn't know what it was.

"Guys," Dana yelled to us looking frightened.

"Dana, what's wrong?" Rachel asked while Dana was running over to us. "Why do you look so frightened, and what is that alarm for?"

"The alarm system is for us," Dana answered.

We all asked at the same time, "What?"

Dana continued to say, "All the workers on this ship works for Ricky."

We all gasped.

Suddenly, everyone except Captain Bert on the ship surrounded us with swords.

"I have had it," Rachel yelled angrily. "I don't care how many people are here. I want to finish what we started and no one is going to stop me."

"Wow, I never knew Rachel had it in her," Dana said looking impressed. "Just remind me to never get on her bad side."

"Then, what is your plan?" Jack asked. "How can we get out of this situation?"

"I don't know," Rachel answered.

"What I think we should do is to fight until we win," Dana said.

"You always like to fight someone," Rachel said. "You always have since after you saw your very first action movie."

"I can't help it," Dana said. "I like action."

"Shadow, Whisper, and I will take the workers on the side of the ship," I said. "Dana, Rachel, and Jack, you take the ones in front of the ship."

"Let's do it," Rachel and Dana said at the same time.

We started the fight when Shadow kicked one of the workers in the face and he fell off the ship. Whisper helped by taking some of the swords that the workers had with her magic making them fly into the air. Shadow and I were able to do the rest. Jack was protecting Dana and Rachel because they had nothing to protect themselves with.

"Rachel up there, the silver ladder," Dana said looking at a ladder on the other side of the ship. "We can go up there and be safe."

"Your right," Rachel agreed with Dana. "We have to hurry so that Jack can take care of them, himself."

Dana and Rachel went up the ladder that was nailed to the side of the ship. Some of the workers tried to follow them, but Rachel kicked them farther down.

When Dana and Rachel got to the top of the ladder, they turned around and saw that the workers were near the top.

"Rachel, I have an idea," Dana said. "You go on that side of the ladder and I'll go on this side."

"Ok," Rachel said. "Now what do we do?"

"Push!" Dana yelled while they started to push the ladder with all their strength.

Then, the nails that were rusted with age, on the ladder started to pop out and the ladder started to tip over while some of the workers were still on it. Dana and Rachel still pushed as hard as they could and when the ladder was weak enough they pushed it harder to make the ladder fall. No one got hurt, but some of the workers fell off the side of the ship.

"Yeah," Dana and Rachel yelled at the same time and slapped each other's hands with grins on their faces. They looked down to see what was happening at the bottom with Jack, but they didn't know that one of the workers was behind them.

The worker pushed Dana off the edge above the ocean, but Rachel caught her and when Dana screamed, Jack heard her. He looked and saw what was happening, so he jumped on a box and started to jump on small ledges that he could reach to get to where Dana and Rachel were. The worker looked at Rachel and pushed her off the edge, but Dana was still holding on to Rachel's hand. Rachel grabbed the edge with one hand and screamed; still holding on to Dana. Jack moved faster.

"Dana, can you hold onto my legs?" Rachel asked. "I need both hands."

"Ok," Dana answered while grabbing Rachel's legs. "Just be careful."

"Say bye, bye," the worker said to Rachel.

Just then, Jack was at the top where Dana, Rachel, and the worker were. When Jack growled the worker looked at him and Jack jumped at the worker to make him fall off the edge into the ocean. While the girls watched him fall, Rachel said, "bye, bye."

When Jack looked over the edge, he saw the girls. When Dana and Rachel saw him they smiled and said at the same time, "Jack!"

"Here," Jack said to Rachel. "Grab my tail and I'll pull you two up."

Rachel grabbed Jack's tail and when he felt her hand, he started to pull as hard as he could. When Rachel got half way up she let go of Jack's tail and got up the rest of the way. Dana let go of Rachel's legs to hold onto the edge, then Rachel and Jack helped Dana get up.

When Dana got up she said, "Thanks, Jack."

"Are you two alright?" Jack asked.

They both answered at the same time, "yeah."

"I think you should help Whisper," Jack said looking at where Whisper was fighting some of the workers by herself. "She looks like she's in trouble. I need to finish some of the workers on the deck."

"You think we should have taken a sword or two?" Dana asked.

"To help Whisper, yeah we should," Rachel answered. "How can we?"

"I think I know," Dana answered. "Follow me."

Dana and Rachel started to jump down onto the boxes to go help Whisper.

When they were near a worker Dana had a grin on her face.

"Stay here," Dana said. "Wait until I say it's ok."

Dana went behind the worker, took two of the swords that were on the side of his belt, and kicked him on the butt that made him fall off the edge.

"Nice," Rachel said coming over to Dana. "You do butt kicking lessons?"

"Very funny," Dana said. "That felt good doing that."

"It was funny," Rachel agreed with Dana. "Why not do it again?"

"Ok," Dana answered, going up to another worker doing the same thing she did with the other worker as she took two more swords from him.

"I liked that," Rachel said.

"Me too," Dana agreed with Rachel while handing her two swords.

When Dana turned around, she saw a worker behind Rachel, and then Dana yelled, "Rachel, behind you!"

Rachel turned around and saw the worker swinging his sword behind his head to strike Rachel, but she went under his feet as he missed. The worker turned around and was about to swing again when Dana came behind him and pocked her sword in the worker's butt. He yelled in pain and Rachel kicked him making him fall over the edge into the ocean.

"Rachel, you ok?" Dana asked, "Are you hurt?"

"I'm fine, Dana," Rachel answered. "Go help Whisper while I take care of these guys."

Dana nodded and started to run to Whisper to help her. Dana took the ones that were behind Whisper so she wouldn't get hurt. Dana pushed some of the workers over the edge of the ship and helped Whisper fight some of the workers she was fighting.

"Thank you, Dana," Whisper said flying around sprinkling dust everywhere to put spells on them and making them fight each other. "But I can handle this; you should stop the captain, but be careful."

Dana started to run up to where Captain Bert was steering the ship and when Captain Bert heard Dana coming he took out a sword. When Dana got to the door she stopped to take a breath. When she looked inside, the captain was lying in wait.

"Why try to fight me, Dana? Even if you defeat my workers, you can't defeat me. Do you know why I'm the captain? It's because I can defeat anyone that gets in my way, so you should just give up and surrender."

"I'd rather not, Captain Bert," Dana answered. "You've never met me before and I don't listen to people too easily."

Dana threw the sword across the room and Captain Bert dodged it, but Dana's plan was to get into the room so she wouldn't get hurt. When Captain Bert was watching the sword, Dana was able to get in the room and act like she was still hiding.

"A sword, Dana?" Captain Bert asked. "That's your plan? Do you think I'm stupid?"

"Yes," Dana answered behind him.

Captain Bert turned around and sliced Dana's arm, but she didn't think about it. Then she ran to the side of him and bit his hand to make him drop the sword. When Captain Bert dropped the sword, they pushed each other until Dana stomped on his foot to give her enough space to trip him into a chair. Dana grabbed the sword to make sure he wouldn't move while pointing it at his neck.

"Now, you won't use my sword on me Dana," Captain Bert said, "You don't have the courage."

Suddenly, Whisper came in the room and Dana asked without looking, "Rachel is that you?"

"It's Whisper," Whisper answered. "Are you ok?"

"Yes, I'm fine," Dana answered back still holding the sword. "Can you help me tie him up?"

"Yes," Whisper answered while tying the captain up.

Then Rachel and Jack came in looking worried.

"Dana, are you alright?" Rachel and Jack asked at the same time. "We heard a lot of noise."

"Yes, I'm fine," Dana answered putting the sword down. "What about you two, or Crystal and Shadow, and what about the workers?"

"Everyone's fine," Jack answered. "We finished fighting the workers."

"Dana," Rachel said looking frightened. "You're bleeding."

"Really?" Dana asked looking at her arm. "I never felt that. Then the captain must have done it when we were fighting."

Rachel went over to Dana and started to bandage her arm.

"Well, what are you going to do with me?" Captain Bert asked. "You can't keep me here forever."

"We can," Dana answered. "But why keep you? We can throw you into the ocean."

"Then I'll just swim to our destination and warn Ricky," Captain Bert said. "I know where he is and I can use my knowledge to get me there."

"Really? I took out your compass, map, weapons, and even if you know how to follow the stars, it's too far," Dana exclaimed. "It will take us one more day to get to our destination, and it will take you at least three or four days in the middle of the ocean."

"Then he'll walk the plank," Rachel said. "Dana's right and we do know how to get there because the captain told us."

Dana and Rachel pushed Captain Bert off the ship. We let Dana and Rachel steer the ship since they knew how to get to our destination.

"That was fun," Dana said. "But I feel like this happened before."

"Why is that, Dana?" Jack asked confused, and then we all looked at Dana confused as well.

"It's this book I read," Dana answered. "A lot of this is what happened in the book, but let's not think about that. We should think of a plan to stop Ricky. I wonder what he's up to."

Chapter 9

"I can't believe they want to still go on this trip," Ricky said angrily. "Just to save you? I had to make all those traps to stop them. Not to have fun and not to make more friends."

"Like I said before," David said. "You can't stop them because they can't be stopped."

"Then if they want a fight, I'll give them one," Ricky said with a grin on his face. "When Dana sees this stone and reads it, she will know who I really am."

"What do you mean?" David asked. "You lied to me?"

"You will see and very soon," Ricky answered.

While Ricky was planning another trap and we were nearing our destination, Robert was still looking for Dana and Rachel.

After Robert and his men searched by the stream, they went back to the ranch so Robert could think of where else to look.

"Where can they be?" Robert asked himself. "I know that Dana would go to the stream to let the horses go free, but why didn't she come back? Johnson, come here."

"Yes, sir," Johnson, Robert's best friend, answered. Johnson was wearing brown cloths like Robert, has light green eyes, and has light brown hair.

"Get me Ricky!" Robert ordered. "He might know something about Dana and Rachel. I know he's been keeping his eye on her for some time."

"Sir, many people have been looking for him," Johnson said. "But we can't find him."

"What?" Robert yelled. "What do you mean you can't find him?"

"He disappeared, sir," Johnson answered. "He has not been seen for a while now."

"How long?" Robert asked angrily.

"About the time that Dana and Rachel went missing," Johnson answered confused. "Why sir, what is it?"

"I think I know where they are," Robert answered. "Get me a helicopter!"

While Robert was waiting for a helicopter we were getting closer to land:

It was night time and I felt as though something bad was going to happen. Everyone was sleeping except Shadow and I woke up suddenly inside the ship.

"What's wrong, Crystal?" Shadow asked concerned. "Or did you feel it to?"

"Yes, I felt it," I answered. "There's a storm coming. We have to warn the others."

Shadow and I started to run onto the deck to warn Dana, Rachel, Jack, and Whisper.

"Dana, Rachel, get out here!" I yelled. "Jack, Whisper, wake up!"

Dana, Rachel, Jack, and Whisper ran out of the Captain's room looking confused and worried.

"What is it?" Dana asked rubbing her eyes.

"I guess you sensed it too," Jack said. "I woke up and felt it. Then I woke Whisper up."

"I sensed it as well," Whisper added. "We were just about to tell Dana and Rachel."

"Tell us what?" Dana asked annoyed. "What's going on?"

"A storm's coming," Jack answered. "And it's near."

Dana and Rachel looked surprised with their mouths open.

"What?" Dana and Rachel asked at the same time.

"We just felt it," Shadow answered. "And now I think it's too late. It's here."

Everyone looked up at the sky when Shadow said that. The light, blue sky was now covered by dark, grey rain clouds. We all heard thunder, and the wind started to blow harder making the ocean move. The ship tilted slightly over and we all had to hang on to something to stop us from falling over. Then the ship tilts slightly over to the other side letting Dana and Rachel run up to the Captain's room. They ran toward the steering wheel to keep the ship from flipping over.

"We have to get out of this storm!" Rachel yelled to Dana. "We can't stay here!"

"I know!" Dana yelled back. "Let's try to steer us away from the storm until it passes."

Dana and Rachel tried to steer as hard as she could away from the storm. Shadow, Jack, Whisper, and I were still on the deck trying not to fall off. Whisper put a force field over us while holding onto me to keep us out of the rain and to not move from side to side.

"How are you doing, Whisper?" I asked. "Can you keep the shield up?"

"I'm doing my best," Whisper answered. "But Dana and Rachel had better hurry. I don't know how long I can keep the shield up."

"I'll go tell Dana," Jack said running up to the Captain's room.

"Wait, Jack!" Shadow yelled.

Jack ran up to Dana and yelled, "Whisper can't hold on any longer. We have to get out of this storm!"

"We're almost there!" Dana yelled while she and Rachel held on to the wheel.

There was a sight of light blue in the sky that they were heading for. Then finally we were out of the storm and into calm seas.

"There, we made it," Dana and Rachel said at the same time.

After the storm passed, we started to head back to our destination. Whisper was so tired from keeping the force field up that she fell asleep on my back. We were near land and almost done with our adventure.

"Land ho," Shadow yelled so everyone could hear him.

"We all see that, Shadow," I said. "But we're not humans or what Dana and Rachel call pirates."

"I'm just having a little fun," Shadow answered.

"I know," I said with a laugh.

"I hope that's the place," Dana said. "I mean, we don't know if it is."

"Well, it's on the map," Rachel answered. "I think it's the right one."

"You really think it is?" Dana asked. "Or, are you thinking what I'm thinking?"

Rachel looked at Dana and nodded with a grin. I thought we were all thinking the same thing. Rachel and Dana said at the same time turning their heads and looking at the map, "It's a trap!"

"I wonder what traps he set for us this time," Dana said. "All his other traps failed."

"What I'm worried about is David," Rachel said. "What if we're too late?"

"Rachel, I'm going to tell you what a very close friend of mine told me every time I said something like that," Dana answered putting her arm around the back of Rachel's neck.

"My friend tells me that we will stop Ricky and save David and to also calm down." Dana said with a bright smile.

"You are right, Dana," Rachel said with a smile. "We will stop Ricky and save David. I shouldn't have a meltdown like you do, so let's go."

"You know," Dana said with a smug look on her face. "You didn't need to say that in front of me or even at all."

"Sorry," Rachel said giggling.

While everyone was getting off the passenger ship Dana asked, "Whisper, can you see if there are any houses, or at least one house?"

Whisper started to fly higher up into the sky, but there were too many clouds in the way for her to see anything.

"Sorry, Dana," Whisper answered. "The clouds were in my way."

"That's ok," Dana said. "I think we should just guess where we go from here."

Jack started to sniff the air and said, "I think we should go this way. I smell something."

"Worth a shot," Rachel answered. "We'll follow Jack."

We all started to follow Jack into a swamp while he kept sniffing the air.

"Jack, can you smell anything?" Rachel asked. "Or is the swamp too damp for you?"

"The swamp is too damp," Jack answered. "I'm sorry, but I can't smell anything else."

"At least you tried, Jack," Dana said. "Thanks anyway."

"We'll just have to wing it then," Rachel suggested. "That's about the only thing we can do."

"Ok," Dana answered. "Then which way should we go?"

"I don't know," Rachel answered. "But, what I don't want around here are alligators, or even crocodiles."

"If we know, Ricky," Dana said, "he's sure to make that happen."

"You will protect me," Rachel said in a terrified voice. "Won't you?"

"I will, Rachel," Dana answered trying to calm her down. "I will, and I promise nothing will happen to you."

"Thanks Dana," Rachel said starting to calm down. "I'm really glad you're with me."

"I was the one who wanted to go on this adventure," Dana said. "Remember, Rachel."

"Yes," Rachel answered. "I do remember, but still. I'm glad you're with me."

"Oh, Rachel," Dana said in a tired voice. "What am I going to do with you?"

"Protect me from the alligators, or crocodiles that are in front of us," Rachel answered running behind Dana.

Everyone was frightened. Especially Rachel who was behind Dana, but we had to get past these creatures. There were three of these creatures that Shadow, Whisper, Jack, and I have never seen before. They had sharp teeth, long thick tails, no fur, small thick legs that are close to the ground. Their bodies had something that Dana and Rachel called scales which look like small, square, or rectangular shapes.

Rachel started to scream when the three creatures were getting closer, but Whisper flew over them and put some of the dust on them. Just like when she did it to us back at the rain forest. One of the creatures said, "We are hungry and want to eat you."

We all stepped backwards to get as far away from the creatures as we could. Jack went in front of us and asked, "Why would you like to eat us?"

"We eat what is on our land," one of the creatures answered. "You are on our land, so we will eat you."

"I won't let that happen," Jack said. "Now let's…"

"Jack don't you even think about it," Dana yelled while everyone looked at her. "Do I need to remind you about last time? You just finished healing. No, you will reopen your wounds. Shadow and Crystal are going to help you this time. Rachel, Whisper, and I will help each other and no one is going to get hurt. Do you all here me?"

None of us wanted to start an argument with Dana, so we all listened to her and were going to help each other. One of the creatures went in back of us to fight with Dana, Rachel, and Whisper while the other two creatures were going to fight Shadow, Jack, and I.

Whisper started the fight by flying over the creature and making it blind with the dust she put on it, but the creature could still smell them. It shook off the extra dust and tried to bite Whisper, but it missed.

"Rachel, I have an idea," Dana said. "Just stay with Whisper."

Rachel nodded and Dana went in front of the creature. It tried to bite her, but Dana moved quickly. Dana started to head for the trees and the creature followed the scent and Rachel understood what Dana was trying to do. Dana was trying to lure the creature deeper into the swamp and get it lost. It worked after a few minutes.

Dana came running and said, "You like my idea?"

Rachel started to giggle and answered, "Yeah."

On our side, one of the creatures tried to bite Shadow's leg, but missed. Then Shadow kicked it in the head. The creature tried it again, but Shadow was too fast and hit it again. The creature backed off so Shadow wouldn't hit it.

The creature tried to bite me, but I was too fast as well. Then Shadow kicked it in the head even harder and made the creature swim away. Dana looked worried about Jack while he and the creature were fighting, but Jack was careful.

When the creature tried to bite Jack, he jumped away and tried to hit it in the eyes with his paws. The creature was smart and backed away before Jack hit it, but when Shadow and I were done fighting the other creature we went beside Jack. Dana, Rachel, and Whisper did the same, but when the creature saw us all together it stopped attacking and swam off.

"Is everyone ok?" Dana asked.

We all answered at the same time smiling at her, "Yes, Dana."

Chapter 10

"That was too close, Jack," Dana said relieved. "It almost got you, and Crystal and Shadow too."

"We know, Dana," Jack said trying to calm her down. "But we can take care of ourselves. You and Rachel did the same thing when you left home."

"I'm sorry everyone," Dana answered looking sad and disappointed. "It's just, when Jack got hurt I thought he was dead and that frightened me. I didn't want anyone else to get hurt."

We all felt sad for Dana and started to curl around her in a hug to comfort her.

"Well, I'm alright Dana," Jack said nuzzling her. "I will be fine, I promise."

"Just you make sure you keep that promise," Dana said with a small smile. "I will make sure you keep that promise as well."

"I wouldn't have it any other way," Jack answered. "Besides, who else will act as my mother?"

"Oh, I don't think you should have said that, Jack," Rachel said giggling. "I think you're going to be in a lot of trouble."

"Yeah," Dana answered giggling while petting Jack. "You're soon going to get it."

We all started to laugh for a few moments, and then we started to go through the swamp. We didn't know where to go and we all felt that we were going the wrong way.

"Are we going in circles?" Dana asked annoyed. "I could have sworn I saw this tree before."

"How can you know that?" Rachel asked. "They all look the same to me."

"Maybe we are going in circles," Whisper answered. "We might not know it, but we might be going the right way."

Everyone was confused.

"This is a lot like when we were in the rain forest," Dana said. "But Whisper helped us. Now we're completely lost."

"Whisper, try to fly higher," I suggested. "Tell us if you see anything."

"That's a good idea, Crystal," Jack said. "It looks clearer now. Maybe Whisper can see something."

Whisper started to fly higher into the sky to see if there was anything up there that she could see.

"Everyone," Whisper yelled. "I can see it and we're going the right way."

Whisper came down and showed us the way through the swamp.

"We've been walking for hours," Dana said. "Are you sure it's this way, Whisper?"

"I'm sure Dana," Whisper answered. "I saw it further ahead."

"Maybe we should rest," Shadow suggested. "It's getting dark out."

"I think Shadow's right, Dana," Rachel agreed with Shadow. "We should make it there in the morning, and we need enough energy…"

"To stop Ricky," Dana interrupted quickly.

Rachel crossed her arms with a little frown looking at Dana. Dana looked a little frightened and asked with a little smile and laughing, "Why are you looking at me like that?"

"Oh, no reason," Rachel answered. "I just like to make you scared."

"I don't think so," Dana said. "You're just a little mad because I interrupted you."

"Yes," Rachel agreed. "But sometimes you just need to watch what you say. It could get you in trouble."

"Ok, ok," Dana said a little irritated. "Let's just go find…"

Dana froze and was looking at an old mining tunnel.

"I think we found him," Rachel said. "He's closer than we think."

"So, we have to go through a dark tunnel?" Whisper asked terrified. "I don't really like dark tunnels."

"Don't worry, Whisper," Shadow answered trying to calm her down. "We'll all go through it together, and we'll stay close so we won't get lost."

"Well, before we pass through the tunnel," I said. "Does anyone have a light?"

Everyone shook their heads answering no. Dana looked troubled.

"Are you alright, Dana?" I asked, but Dana didn't listen. Instead, she was thinking about something that made us invisible, and then I asked again, "Dana?"

"Oh, ah, what did you say?" Dana asked shaking her head and everyone was looking at her. "I wasn't listening, sorry."

"I asked if you were alright," I answered. "You never answered me."

"Oh, yeah, yeah, I'm, I'm fine, I'm fine," Dana answered acting different and a little afraid. "It's just, this is so familiar."

"What?" Rachel asked. "Do mean the book you keep mentioning? Did it have a tunnel as well?"

"Yes," Dana answered. "It's almost like it's..., never mind. I'll tell you after we defeat Ricky. So, does anyone have a light?"

We all looked at Dana with straight faces.

"What?" Dana asked.

"We already answered that question," Shadow answered. "Or did you not hear it?"

"I didn't hear it," Dana answered. "Sorry."

"That's alright, Dana," Jack said. "We just need to find something to..., Whisper?"

"Yes," Whisper answered. "What is it?"

"Can you make yourself into a light?" Jack asked. "You can guide us through the tunnel."

"I think I can," Whisper answered. "Hold on."

We all watched Whisper turn herself into a bright light by throwing some of her dust into the air, letting it fall on her.

"Alright," Whisper said glowing like a bright star in the sky. "Are we all ready to go through the tunnel?"

"I thought you were scared to pass through the tunnel?" Shadow asked. "What made you change your mind?"

"I realize that I will be fine," Whisper answered still glowing brightly. "I have my friends with me."

"That's good," Rachel said. "So can you be brave enough to go first, then?"

Whisper looked terrified and started to lose her light, like house lights slowly dimming.

"Nice Rachel. Whisper is starting to turn off," Dana said.

Then she looked at Whisper. "Don't worry Whisper. I'll go first and you just have to give me enough light so I can see, ok?"

"I will like that Dana," Whisper answered in relief turning back into a bright light again. "Thank you so much."

Chapter 11

We started to pass through the tunnel and it started to get darker, but with Whisper shinning like a bright star; it was clear for us to see.

"I feel like we're going down," Dana said puzzled. "Not straight."

"Yeah, I feel it to," Rachel agreed with Dana. "Why is that?"

"Maybe, Ricky's hideout is under-ground," Jack answered. "Or maybe it's a trick, and his hideout is really the house on the surface and not underground."

"Then shouldn't we go back?" I asked.

"No, we shouldn't. His hideout might be here," Dana answered. "When we get out of the tunnel, Jack and Whisper can go back to see if that house is his hideout. If it is or isn't, come back here and tell us."

When we got out of the tunnel, Jack and Whisper went back into it.

"I guess this is Ricky's hideout," Rachel said looking at a stone in the middle of the room with empty space around it. There was different equipment on the sides and some cells in-between some of the equipment.

"Rachel, Dana," a voice shouted out. "Is that you?"

Dana and Rachel said at the same time, "it's David!"

Dana and Rachel started to run over to where David was and Shadow and I followed. Then Dana looked at the stone and stopped running, but Rachel didn't notice and kept running toward David. Dana started walking toward the stone with a puzzled look on her face and was oblivious to any sound that tried to reach her, like she was deaf.

"It can't be," Dana said to herself looking down at the stone. "It shouldn't be."

While Dana was staring at the stone, Rachel was near the cell David was in.

"David, are you ok?" Rachel asked frightened.

"I'm fine," David answered. "Can you get me out of this cell?"

"I think so," Rachel answered thinking of some way to get him out.

"Crystal, Shadow, can you try to kick the bars out of place? David, move out of the way."

Shadow and I walked to the cell and kicked the bars out of place for David to get out.

"Thank you, Rachel," David said. "Thank you Stallion."

"My name is Shadow, and you're welcome," Shadow explained, while David was looking at him as if to have never seen a horse talk before.

"Are you alright?" Rachel asked David while he stared at Shadow with a frightened look. "David, what's wrong?"

"So it's true. You really can talk," David said. "I thought Ricky was playing a joke on me."

"No, it's true," Rachel corrected him. "How did you know Shadow could talk?"

"Ricky's been watching you girls from everywhere," David answered. "We have to get out before he comes back. He said he has a surprise for you girls, and I don't think it's good."

"I don't think so either," Rachel agreed with David.

"Alright, then let's go Dana," Rachel said suddenly wondering where Dana was and didn't know she was near the stone. "Dana?"

"What's wrong with Dana?" David asked while we all looked at her.

Rachel answered, "I don't know."

Then Rachel called out Dana's name again. Dana gave no answer just as if she were deaf.

"I do remember Ricky saying something about Dana," David said. "Something about her knowing what that stone is."

"Maybe, it has something to do with the book she read," Rachel thought out loud.

"What's about the stone that's so interesting to you Dana?" she shouted.

Rachel, David, Shadow, and I walked over to the stone and looked at it. On the stone was writing, but I couldn't read it for it was a different language that I've never seen before.

"Dana, why are you so interested in this stone?" Rachel asked, but still no answer from her. "Dana, now you're starting to make me mad, so how about you wake up from this trance."

Dana gave no answer still, and I could see Rachel starting to get angry.

"Dana, wake up!" Rachel yelled while making Dana shake her head.

"Wha... what, what, what did you say?" Dana asked holding her head. "I didn't hear you."

"Finally, if I didn't know you I would think you were in a trance or something," Rachel said in relief. "What I asked is why you are so interested in the stone?"

"Oh, it's because..."

"The stone is from the book," Ricky answered interrupting Dana while we all looked behind us to see him.

Then, Dana and Rachel said at the same time, "Ricky!"

"Hello, Dana and Rachel," Ricky said with a smile. "I was just waiting for you, and here you are."

"What do you want, Ricky?" Dana asked. "What's your plan, or is the stone of Albemore your plan?"

"Very clever," Ricky answered. "But, you're too late. For I have started it before you tried to free Crystal and Shadow. All I had to do was to kidnap David as bait for you to fall into my trap."

"What do you mean?" David asked. "You lied to me, even though Dana knew what that stone was."

"I lied to you, so you wouldn't tell them," Ricky answered. "I knew Dana knows about the stone of Albemore and I wanted to know if she could recognize it.

The story about that stupid Robert was false, so I could keep the true story."

"My father is not stupid," Dana said angrily. "He's much smarter than you are. We're going to stop you, whatever it takes."

Ricky started to laugh in a devilish way. "You think you can stop me" Ricky said. "How will you stop me? The stone is lit and you know exactly what that means, Dana."

Dana looked at him with her mouth slightly opened, and then turned to the stone.

"Dana, what does that mean?" Rachel asked. "That makes no sense to me, and I want to know what's going on right now."

"It's hard to explain, Rachel," Dana said looking down at the stone. "I don't know where to start."

"I don't care if it takes you all year," Rachel said. "I want to know now."

"Firstly, you're the one who tells me to calm down," Dana said. "I think I will tell you to calm down."

"Dana, please tell us," I asked. "We would also like to know what's going on here."

"It's a long story," Dana answered. "But, I might as well tell you."

"In the book," Dana started to say. "The stone has magical powers that can change or redo history."

"What?" Rachel asked with a surprised face.

Dana started to think how she could define what she said.

"Well, it's like this," Dana exclaimed. "If something happened a long time ago that had something to do with the stone and someone reactivated it, the stone would redo time. They can make it happen again, but with different people."

"Then does that mean that it's doing the same thing?" Rachel asked. "But, with us?"

"Yes," Dana answered. "But, that's only because Ricky reactivated the stone causing it to redo history. That means we're in Albemore, like in the book."

"So, that's what you were taking about," David said looking at Ricky. "But why need Dana here?"

Everyone turned to look at him.

"Why not let Dana tell you," Ricky answered. "She knows everything about me and the stone."

"So, all you want me to do is tell them everything while you watch?" Dana asked. "How about you tell them instead of me, or else you might not know what to do and get all the information out of me."

"I do know everything," Ricky yelled angrily. "I'm Borabus, and my ancestor was Corabus which you should know."

"No, that can't be," Dana said frightened. "You can't be him."

"Oh, but I am," Ricky answered. "And do you know who you are?"

Dana thought for a moment about what Ricky asked. She looked puzzled about it until she looked surprised.

"Now you know," Ricky said after he saw Dana's surprised expression. "You're the ancestor of Aura. Now, prepare for your end."

Chapter 12

Ricky's workers came out and surrounded us.

"No, that can't be," Dana said with an expressionless look on her face holding her head. "I can't be her. Although it makes sense, I just can't be her."

"Dana," Rachel said. "What's wrong? Just because you're the ancestor of someone who did this before doesn't mean you can freak out. We're surrounded by Ricky's workers, so snap out of it. Just tell me what the stone can do!"

"What do you mean?" Dana asked.

"What I mean is, can that stone do anything bad or something?" Rachel asked.

"Yes," Dana answered. "Really bad."

"Then, what?" Rachel asked. "What can it do?"

Dana took a deep breath as if she lost some of it.

"On the stone, it say's..." Dana answered then stopped.

"What?" Rachel asked. "It say's what?"

"It says that whosoever defeats him," Dana answered, "Shall be known as the king or queen of the stars. They will have both body and soul put into the stars and will be seen night after night. If they shall fail, evil shall rule the world."

Rachel looked at Dana with a strange face as if she never heard anything like that before.

"Well, let's not let that happen," Rachel said. "Try to find a way to stop this, or is there already a way to stop this?"

"There is," Dana answered. "There are two ways."

"Then, what are they?" Rachel asked.

"We either stop Ricky and save the world, or burn it in fire," Dana answered.

"What do you mean?" Rachel asked.

"We push the stone into a fire," Dana answered.

Rachel looked at Dana like she was crazy.

"What?" Dana asked. "Why are you staring at me like that?"

"Oh, no reason," Rachel answered. "But, now what can we do? Ricky has us trapped, unless we fight."

"We might need to do that," Shadow answered.

Then, all of a sudden Jack and Whisper came and surprised the workers and said, "We'll help Dana and Rachel. Crystal you help Shadow, and be careful."

"Good," Ricky said. "Now the gang's all here. Attack!"

All the workers started to run toward us and tried to get us. Shadow and I kicked them while Jack bit them and Whisper blinded them.

"Dana, what do we do?" Rachel asked. "How can we help?"

"We have to look at the stone," Dana answered. "There's an incantation or something that might give us powers to protect us, but only for a short time."

"Ok," Rachel said. "Then, read."

Dana started to read the stone as fast as she could. I didn't understand how she could read the stone.

"Rachel, read this with me," Dana said. "I think this is the one."

"How can I?" Rachel asked. "I can't read it."

"Repeat after me," Dana answered. She started to speak in a strange language, and then started to glow bright yellow.

"What the…" Rachel said in amazement.

"Wow," Dana said still glowing. "This is cool."

Suddenly, one of Ricky's workers tried to attack Dana, but the glow around her shielded her and knocked the worker out.

"Wow," Rachel said. "How can I get that?"

"Say the incantation like I did," Dana answered. "That's how you get this glow."

Rachel said the incantation and started to glow like Dana. They both started to fight by having the shield around them, stopping every attack.

All of us kept fighting until I saw Ricky running toward the stone. I saw that he was reading it, and then he started to glow bright yellow like Dana and Rachel. Then, he started to head towards them.

"Shadow," I said. "Look at Ricky, he's glowing and heading towards the girls."

"Your right," Shadow said looking at Ricky. "Let's try to warn them."

Shadow and I started to gallop over to Dana and Rachel trying to get past Ricky's workers.

"Dana, Rachel," I yelled. "Look behind you."

They turned around after they were done and saw Ricky glowing like them.

"Hello girls," Ricky said with a smug on his face.

"He's mad," Rachel said.

"What gave you that idea?" Dana asked giggling.

Ricky took out a sword, and then Dana took two swords from one of the workers and kicked him on the butt.

"Nice," Rachel said. "You do butt kicking lessons?"

"You said that before," Dana answered.

"I know," Rachel said. "I can't help it."

"Here you go," Dana said giving one of the swords to Rachel. "Let's finish this once and for all."

They were just about to fight when all of a sudden, a helicopter arrived and humans jumped out of it holding onto ropes.

"What the…" Dana, Rachel, and Ricky said at the same time.

Then, I saw Robert when he landed on the ground. He was leading the other humans.

"Dad!" Dana said with a puzzled face and still glowing bright yellow. "What are you doing here?"

"I was going to ask you the same question," Robert answered. "Why are you glowing? Why didn't you come back after you let the horses free? Why are Rachel and Ricky glowing? Why are there wild animals everywhere? What's going on?"

"Not now Dad, it's a long story," Dana answered. "We didn't come back because Ricky…"

"Was trying to help them," Ricky said interrupting Dana.

"That's not what happened at all," I said. "You know that Ricky."

Robert and the other humans looked surprised and confused when I talked.

"How can that horse talk?" Robert asked turning toward Dana.

"That's another long story…" Dana said until Ricky grabbed her holding the sword at her neck.

Then Ricky said, "That you won't hear about, Robert."

"Let her go Ricky!" Robert demanded. "Why don't we talk about this instead of hurting someone?"

"No," Ricky answered. "I've had enough of listening to you. Now, you either let me go on that helicopter or I will hurt Dana."

"You know, I've had it with you Ricky," Whisper said. "You are going to let her go right now or… or I'll…"

Suddenly, Whisper started to glow light blue and started to grow into a normal sized horse. Instead of white hair, she had blue hair with long blue wings, but her mane and tail were still black. She flew into the air and started to make the warehouse dark and grabbed Dana.

"Thanks Whisper," Dana said when Whisper put her down.

"Dana," Rachel said running over to her and Whisper with everyone else behind her. Rachel and Robert asked at the same time, "Are you alright?"

"I'm fine," Dana answered and turned to Whisper and hugged her. "I guess you finally broke that spell off you."

"Yes," Whisper said and Dana stopped hugging her. "Yes I did."

"I will ask questions later," Robert said and then the bright yellow light on Dana, Rachel, and Ricky disappeared.

"I guess our powers are gone," Rachel said. Dana said disappointedly, "I liked those powers."

"No!" Ricky yelled. "None of this was supposed to happen. I was supposed to rule the world."

"Oh, yeah?" Dana asked. "Did you finish the book? At the end of it, the bad guy loses."

"Well then," Ricky said going near a lever and pulling it back. "This will be different."

Suddenly, the warehouse started to break apart, opening up fire underneath the ground near the stone.

"Attack!" Ricky yelled to his workers.

They started to surround us until Whisper blew ice out of her wings freezing them.

"Wow," Dana and Rachel said at the same time staring at Whisper.

"What?" Whisper asked. "That was one of my powers I had before that spell was put on me."

Then, we all walked toward Ricky and Ricky backed up near the hole with fire in it.

"No," Ricky said. "This isn't the end for me."

"Want to bet?" Shadow and I asked at the same time and then we both kicked Ricky and the stone into the fire while he was yelled out, "Nooooo."

Then, the whole warehouse started to fall apart shaking the ground.

"We need to get out of here," David yelled.

"Everyone through the tunnel," Jack yelled.

We all started to run through the tunnel and out of there before it fell to the ground.

We all looked back as the warehouse collapsed and I saw my parents in the distance far away, but they didn't come to see if I was alright. I started to think if there was something missing that I forgot about.

Suddenly, light came down from the sky. Shadow and I started to float in the air and started to go up toward the sky.

I remembered what Dana said.

"Dana, what's happening?" Rachel asked. "What's going on?" "Remember what the stone said," Dana answered while everyone was watching Shadow and me. "Whoever stop's him shall have both body and soul in the stars and will be seen night after night forever."

Shadow and I went into the stars and became constellations. They could see us looking down at them and I finally realized why things happen for a reason. I was born into this world to help Dana and Rachel and to help save the world. Now, I'm a legend and I'm proud of it.

"So, I guess that's it then," Dana said having a tear run down her face. "I'm always going to remember this for the rest of my life."

"Yeah, me too," Rachel said also having a tear run down her face. "But one more thing, do we have to go through the desert again?"

Then, everyone started laughing.

Epilogue

After Shadow and I became constellations, my parents went to the herd to tell them what happened to us. They were all sad for us, but will always see us in the stars forever. My parents stayed and watched over the herd. David, Jack, and Whisper stayed with Dana and Rachel to be a happy family. But Shadow and I know that we'll never be forgotten. Dana and Robert became closer as a father and daughter should be. Robert stopped catching lots of wild horses and instead he started a sanctuary to protect them so they could roam free. Dana liked that the most and helped him save the horses along with Rachel.

"So Whisper gave everyone the ability to talk," Robert said after Dana and Rachel told him what happened. "You had to save David from Ricky too."

"Yeah," Dana said. "Crazy story."

"It was weird," Rachel said agreeing with Dana. "But we saved David and the world from evil."

"I still loved it," Dana said. "It was so awesome."

"Maybe you should write a book about it," David suggested. "I bet it will be a big hit."

"David, it's already out there," Whisper said correcting him. "There's a book on what happened a long time ago."

"Yes there is," Dana said. "Like I said before during the journey, I read a book that was similar to what happened to all of us, except for dad coming in a helicopter. That was new and wasn't in the book."

"Really?" David asked puzzled. "What's it called?"

"Trip to Albemore," Lynn and Rachel said at the same time.

"Albevoe," David said trying to pronounce it.

"No, Albemore" Dana said giggling.

"Albadore," David said trying to pronounce it again.

"No, Albemore" Rachel said giggling.

"Albanoe," David tried again.

"No," Dana and Rachel said at the same time laughing and fell to the floor. They laughed so hard and couldn't talk that everyone started to laugh.

As for Shadow and me, we will be happy as constellations. We'll be able to watch over everyone, especially, all of our friends. We'll always see them look up at us every night.

There's also one more thing I forgot to mention. Shadow and I are right next to the horses that saved the world a long time ago. So, now I hope you understand why things happen for a reason. All you really need to do is to have courage and to never give up of fighting for the world.

CPSIA information can be obtained
at www.ICGtesting.com
Printed in the USA
BVHW041446081022
648927BV00008BA/650